Barbie™

The Holiday Gift

A
FUN WORKS
SHIMMER BOOK

One sparkling winter day, Barbie hurried to the
home of Mrs. Jenson, the town seamstress, to try on
her gown for the Holiday Snowflake Parade.
Barbie had been voted the parade queen,
and her friends were the princesses.
They were going to ride together
on a float in the parade.
"Your dress is almost
finished," Mrs. Jenson said, as
she led Barbie into her sunny
sewing room. "Oh, it's lovely,"
Barbie exclaimed when she saw
the dress of rich, green satin. "I
can't wait to try it on."

As Barbie slipped into her gown, a pretty girl peeked through the doorway. "Laura, come and meet Barbie," said Mrs. Jenson as she pinned the gown's hem. "Barbie, this is my granddaughter, Laura. She's spending the holidays with me."

"Hello, Laura," Barbie said, smiling. But Laura ducked her head and slipped away.

"Laura is so shy," Mrs. Jenson sighed. "I'm afraid she won't make friends or have a good time while she's here."

Just then, Barbie heard Laura playing the piano in the living room and singing in a sweet, clear voice.

As she listened, Barbie had a wonderful idea. When her fitting was finished, she slipped into the living room and sat beside Laura.

"Laura," she asked, "will you ride on the float with me and my friends and sing in the parade?"

"Oh, I-I'm not sure," Laura said, hesitantly. "I-I don't even have a gown to wear."

"Please think about it," Barbie said. "And," she added with a smile, "keep practicing that pretty song—just in case you decide to join us."

Barbie hurried to meet her friends at the Sweet Shoppe. "I have a wonderful idea," she told them as she sat down.

"That's terrific!" Midge exclaimed when Barbie finished sharing her idea.

"Laura's singing would make the parade special," Skipper agreed.

"She'd make lots of new friends, too," added Teresa.

"Let's sing a song together first, so Laura won't feel so embarrassed," Christie suggested.

"That's a great idea!" Barbie exclaimed. "Let's go ask the Mayor's permission!"

Barbie and her friends hurried to Town Hall. "What can I do for my favorite Snowflake Queen and Princesses today?" The Mayor asked, welcoming them into her office.

"We have a great idea for the Holiday Snowflake Parade," Barbie answered. "May we show you?" The Mayor nodded. Barbie and her friends began to sing. When they finished, the Mayor applauded.

"Of course you can sing on the float," she exclaimed. We'll add microphones so everyone can hear you. Thank you for a lovely idea."

"Now, I just have to encourage Laura to sing, too," said Barbie happily as they left the Mayor's office. Then suddenly, she stopped. "Oh dear, I forgot!" she exclaimed. "Laura doesn't have a gown!"

"Design one for her, Barbie!" Midge suggested. "You design dresses for us all the time!"

"All right!" Barbie agreed. "Let's go choose the fabric." At the Fashion Sew Shop, everyone helped Barbie choose and pay for some lush, pink velvet. "This color will look beautiful on Laura," she said.

Next, everyone went to Barbie's house and watched Barbie design Laura's gown. Then Barbie telephoned Mrs. Jenson to explain her idea.

"What a sweet surprise!" Mrs. Jenson exclaimed. "I'll make Laura's gown and bring it to Town Hall when she and I come to help you dress for the parade."

"Is Laura practicing?" Barbie asked.

"Yes," Mrs. Jenson answered. "I think she wants to sing in the parade, if she can get over her shyness."

"Maybe the gown will help," Barbie said.

"I'm sure it will," Mrs. Jenson replied.

On the day of the parade, everyone gathered at the Town Hall. Mrs. Jenson and Laura bustled in carrying Barbie's gown and a large box. After Barbie slipped into her gown, she handed the box to Laura. When Laura saw the dress inside, her eyes sparkled with excitement.

"We want you to sing, and we thought you should have a gown that is as beautiful as your voice," Barbie explained.

Laura gazed at the gown. "Thank you," she said softly. "I'll try to sing my best so you will all be proud of me."

Soon, everyone was seated on the Queen's
float, and the parade began moving down
Main Street past the cheering townspeople.
At the town square, the parade stopped
so Barbie and her friends could sing
to everyone.

"Now, we have a special
surprise," Barbie announced.
"Our new friend, Laura, is
going to sing."

"This song is my gift
to all my new friends,
and especially for Barbie,"
Laura said softly. Then
she started to sing. No
one spoke or moved as
Laura's voice sang
out, sweet and
clear as a bell.

When Laura's song ended, the crowd cheered wildly. Barbie and the others crowded around Laura.

"Thank you, Barbie," Laura said as Barbie hugged her. "You not only gave me new friends, you helped me overcome my shyness. Those are the best gifts I've ever received."

"You gave those gifts to yourself, Laura, by sharing your voice." Barbie replied. "And what's more, you also gave all of us a very special holiday memory."